To Jay, paddler of river and wave M.J.
To Ruth and Mark A.J.

Text copyright © 2000. Mary Joslin. Original edition published in English
under the title **The Shore Beyond** by Lion Publishing plc, Oxford, England.
Copyright © Lion Publishing plc 2000.

North American Edition published by Good Books, 2000. All rights reserved.

THE SHORE BEYOND
Copyright © 2000 by Good Books, Intercourse, PA 17534
International Standard Book Number: 1-56148-316-8
Library of Congress Catalog Card Number: 00-030844

Library of Congress Cataloging-in-Publication Data

Joslin, Mary
    The shore beyond / Mary Joslin ; illustrated by Alison Jay. --
North American ed.
        p.cm.
    Summary: As Little Clara grows up, she leaves her familiar
world for more distant places in search of something that will make
her spirit dance.
    ISBN 1-56148-316-8
    [1. Growth--Fiction. 2. Self-realization--Fiction.] I. Jay, Alison, ill.
II. Title.

PZ7.J786 Sh 2000
[E]--dc21
                                                            00-030844

The Shore Beyond

Mary Joslin

Illustrated by Alison Jay

Good Books
Intercourse, PA 17534
800/762-7171

When Clara was little, she loved most of all to walk down to the lakeside with her father each morning. She watched as he pushed his heavy rowing-boat out into the calm violet water and set off for his day's work.

In the evening, she waited beside the door of their home and looked for his return under a darkening sky. Every night, when he came home, she asked the same question.

'When can I come with you to the shore beyond? I can barely see it from here.'

'When you are older,' was her father's reply.

Summers came and winters passed. On a bright spring day, Clara at last took her place at the oars and pulled the boat out onto the lake.

'This is such a great adventure,' she cried.

Delightedly she gazed at the vastness of the open
water and watched the flocks of birds wheeling
overhead. With every stroke, she was taking the
boat closer to the place she so longed to reach.

Every day, Clara helped her father with the rowing.
   'This boat is very heavy when it is laden down with passengers and all their baggage,' she complained.
   'It is hard work,' agreed her father. 'We ferry people to and fro as they make their living, and in this way we make ours.'

'I just wish there was more to life than making a living,' the girl grumbled.

Her father turned to look at her. 'There is the good companionship of our passengers,' he said calmly, 'and the loveliness of the place we live in.'

But Clara began to dream.

'I'm going to save the money I earn,' she told her friends. 'Then I shall go on a journey of discovery. I shall take my own boat down the river that flows out of this lake. Who knows what I may find?'

Her friends looked at her admiringly. 'You are brave, Clara,' they said.

But only one came up to her afterwards: Miriam, the basket-weaver's daughter.

'I have an idea,' she said. 'My father told me that, when he was a boy, he wove a basket and made it into a tiny boat for himself and travelled a little way down the river. I'm sure he will help us to do the same, and then we can travel together.'

All through the winter evenings they worked
together, each crafting a tiny coracle from woven
willow. They covered the basket frames with heavy
canvas that would keep out even the tiniest drop of water.
As spring came around, they shaped paddles from well-
seasoned cherry wood.

On days when they were not needed for work, the girls
began to try out their tiny boats.

At first they sculled them through the quiet waters at the
edge of the lake. Then they went out a little further.

At last they ventured into the slithering current of the glassy
river and laughed with delight as the water swept them along.

That evening, as they trudged back up
the river bank with their boats, their minds
were made up: 'We are quite grown-up
enough to leave home,' they said.
'When summer comes, we will go
down the river.'

The journey was as exciting as they had dreamed. Their coracles danced among tumbling silver waves and swirled in deep green eddies. The water grabbed at their boats and threatened to pull them under… but Clara and Miriam were too quick, too strong, too clever.

'What fun we're having!' they cried.

'I can ride the waves better than you,' Miriam called to Clara.

So they paddled on the playful waters, day after day, till it seemed they knew every ripple.

One night, as the silver moon sailed among the clouds, Clara sighed. 'I long to travel even further,' she said. 'There must be more to see.'

After a time, the river left the mountains behind. The girls found tiny hamlets in the hills and quiet villages on the gently rolling plain.

Then, at a place where the river fanned out around dozens of tiny islands, they found a bright and busy town. Miriam set about exploring its streets while Clara paddled through the backwaters. They met again by the bank to talk of their discoveries. Miriam looked wistful. 'I have met a basket weaver here, a friend of my family,' she said. 'She has offered to let me stay with her. I have enjoyed the adventure which brought us here. Now I want to settle down and follow the trade I learned from my father. There are so many things I will be able to do here.'

Clara watched as Miriam pulled her battered coracle higher up on the bank.

'Show me the house where you will be living,' she replied, 'for you are my friend, and I will always want to know how to find you. But for now, I want to travel on.'

So they parted. Clara's journey now took her to the sea. Beyond the estuary, the foaming waves picked up her little boat and rolled her in to shore. Time after time she paddled out, and let the waves dance her back.

'If I paddle hard enough, I can go beyond the breakers,'
she thought to herself as she urged her tiny boat through
the foaming sea. But when she had done so, she stopped;
the vast ocean seemed too big for her to travel.

'How can I go still further?' she asked an old sailor she met on the harbour.

'Where do you want to go?' was his reply. 'There are plenty of sailing-boats here, and, if you want, you can travel on any one of them to the lands beyond.'

He told her of the places he had seen, and the wonders to be found.

'But in the end,' he said, 'it is all the same. Everywhere there are people simply going to and fro, making the best of where they are and getting on with those they meet.'

'Everywhere?' asked Clara.

'Everywhere,' he replied. After a moment's pause he went on. 'And everywhere, there are people like you and me, who believe that there must be something more to find.'

Together they watched the sun setting over the purple
sea. From where the waves broke on the sandy shore to the
far horizon there stretched a path of gold.

'Look,' she said. 'That is where I want to go: to where
earth touches heaven... where, beyond the everyday things,

I can find something even greater that will make my spirit dance.'

    She turned to face the old man. 'You have lived a long time,' she said. 'Can you tell me how to reach that shore beyond?'

He smiled kindly at her. 'You may choose to be a traveller, or you may choose to settle down,' he said, 'for your life itself is the journey. But in all you do, live as you would want to on that distant shore. One day you will reach the place you long for, and you will know in your heart that it has for long years been your home.'

FEB -- 2013